Richard Scarry's
A Day at the Fire Station

First published in the USA by Random House in 2003
This edition first published in the UK by HarperCollins Children's Books in 2015
Copyright © 2003 by the Richard Scarry Corporation

3 5 7 9 10 8 6 4 2

ISBN: 978-0-00-757495-7

www.harpercollins.co.uk

Printed and bound in China

Richard Scarry's
A Day at the Fire Station

"Wonderful!" replies Chief Smoky.

Drippy and Sticky, the painters,
pull up in front of the Busytown fire station.
"We're here to paint the station!"
says Drippy.

"But please don't park your paint truck in front of the station doors," Smoky says. "We firefighters have to be able to drive out at ANY time."

After parking their paint truck
out of the way, Drippy and Sticky
enter the fire station.

"Wow! What a nifty place!" says Drippy.

The firefighters are busy cleaning their fire engines. "We firefighters like to keep our engines nice and clean, so please be careful not to get any paint on them," says Smoky.

"Aye-aye, sir!" replies Sticky.

Drippy covers a fire engine with a big cloth so that it won't get dripped on. Sticky opens the cans of paint.

Drippy begins to paint the fire station ceiling pink.
Sticky starts to paint the fire station poles in candy stripes.

Oops! Drippy's cloth seems to have slipped off the fire engine.

"My red fire engine!" shouts Smoky. "It's pink!"

"Don't worry," says Drippy. "We'll have your fire engine cleaned up in no time."

But instead of rubbing off, the wet paint smears in long streaks. What a mess!

RRRINNG! RRRINNG! sounds a loud bell. It's the fire station alarm!

The firefighters sleeping in the dormitory upstairs leap from their beds and slide down the poles to the engines below.

"Oh, no!" shout Drippy and Sticky.
"Oh, no!" shout the firefighters,
covered in candy-stripe paint.

But stained uniforms or no, the brave firefighters jump into their boots, grab their coats and helmets, and charge out of the fire station aboard their red – and pink – fire engines. WWWRRRR! CLANG! CLANG!

"Well," says Drippy, "now that the firefighters are gone, perhaps we can get our painting done."

The firefighters have been called out to a traffic accident. Cecelia's cement mixer bumped into Horace's honey truck and knocked over Farmer Hal's haywagon. What a gooey mess!

Thank goodness for the firefighters! They will have everything cleaned up in no time.

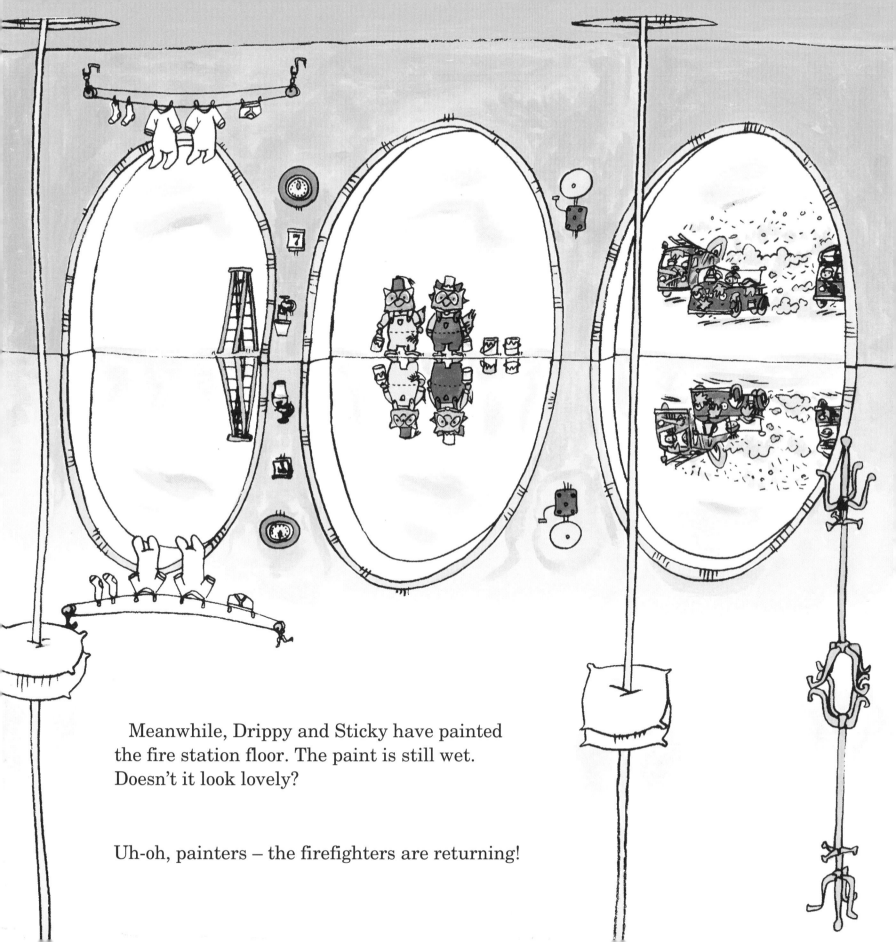

Meanwhile, Drippy and Sticky have painted
the fire station floor. The paint is still wet.
Doesn't it look lovely?

Uh-oh, painters – the firefighters are returning!

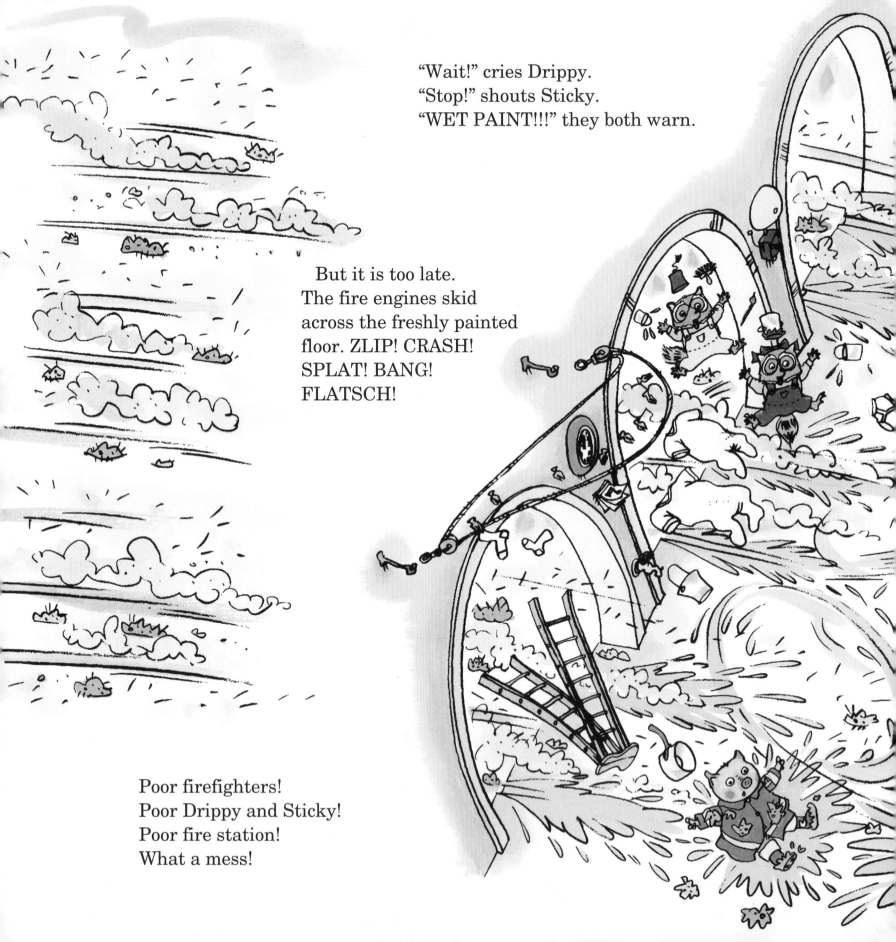

"Wait!" cries Drippy.
"Stop!" shouts Sticky.
"WET PAINT!!!" they both warn.

But it is too late.
The fire engines skid
across the freshly painted
floor. ZLIP! CRASH!
SPLAT! BANG!
FLATSCH!

Poor firefighters!
Poor Drippy and Sticky!
Poor fire station!
What a mess!

Straw and cement
and honey are
EVERYWHERE.

Smoky picks up
a hose and sprays
out the fire station.
SWWIIIIIIIIISH!
SWWOOOOOSH!

Suddenly, there is another alarm.
This time, it's a fire!

The firefighters throw all their equipment
into the fire engines and are off to the rescue.

Look! It's a fire at Vesuvio's Peppery Pizza Parlour!
The firefighters quickly hook up the pumper engine
to the fire hydrant and bravely rush inside.

The fire is in the oven! (It's a burnt pizza.)
Hurry, firefighters!
With a spray of water from the hose, the fire is put out.

To thank the firefighters, Vesuvio invites
them all to a big pizza lunch. Isn't he nice?

Meanwhile, Drippy and Sticky have finished repainting the fire station.

The firefighters bring Drippy and Sticky a takeaway pizza, and wash their fire engines OUTSIDE the fire station while the fresh paint dries. Aren't they thoughtful?

Just then, Tammy Tapir drives up
in her strawberry jam truck.
"Can anyone please tell me how
to get to the motorway from here?"
Tammy asks the firefighters.

Uh-oh. Isn't that Roger Rhino's
wrecking crane coming?
Hey, slow down there, Roger!

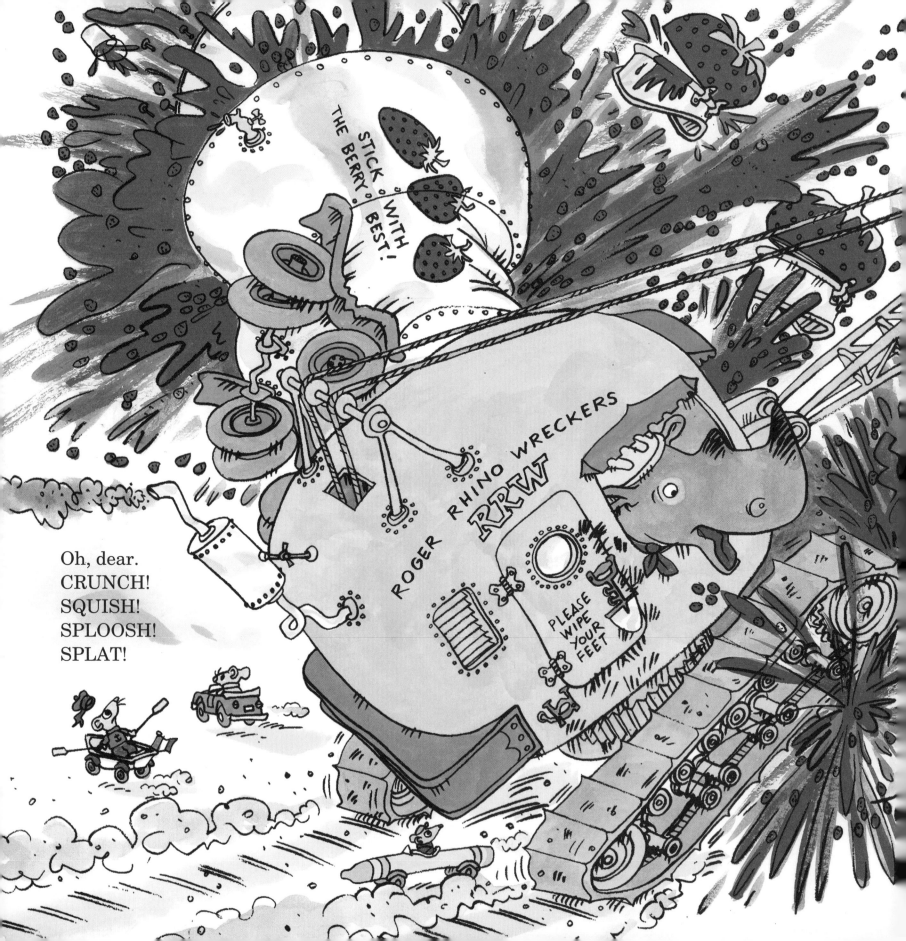

Oh, dear.
CRUNCH!
SQUISH!
SPLOOSH!
SPLAT!

Nice work, Roger!

"Goodness, I'm awfully sorry about this," says Roger, apologising. "Oh, don't worry," says Smoky with a sigh. "We'll have this cleaned up in no time. It's all in a firefighter's day at the fire station."

The wonderful world of
Richard Scarry

Enjoy these classic Richard Scarry books: